THE FOXWOOD TREASURY

Written and Illustrated by
Cynthia and Brian Paterson

HUTCHINSON
London Sydney Auckland Johannesburg

To our three lovely sons – William, Charles and Henry

First published in 1997

3 5 7 9 10 8 6 4

This edition © Hutchinson Children's Books 1997
Text © Cynthia Paterson 1985, 1986, 1987, 1988
Illustrations © Brian Paterson 1985, 1986, 1987, 1988
Licensed by Gresham Marketing

Cynthia and Brian Paterson have asserted their right under
the Copyright, Designs and Patents Act, 1988,
to be identified as the author and illustrator of this work

First published in the United Kingdom in 1997 by
Hutchinson Children's Books
Random House UK Limited
20 Vauxhall Bridge Road, London SW1V 2SA

Random House Australia (Pty) Limited
20 Alfred Street, Milsons Point, Sydney
New South Wales 2061, Australia

Random House New Zealand Limited
18 Poland Road, Glenfield
Auckland 10, New Zealand

Random House South Africa (Pty) Limited
Endulini, 5A Jubilee Road, Parktown 2193, South Africa

Random House UK Limited Reg. No. 954009

A CIP catalogue record for this book is available from the British Library

ISBN: 0 09 176579 X

Printed in Hong Kong

CONTENTS

INTRODUCTION

IT ALL BEGAN WITH Willy Hedgehog, who is a bit like me, really; the rest came from Cynthia's childhood memories of country life. One day I asked her if she would like to write a story about some characters I was developing for a book idea and although she had never envisaged a career as a children's author she had a go. Six books later there is a whole village of personalities who have crossed over from the animal world to emulate the characters of everyday folk we all recognise about us.

It is a delight to watch Harvey, Rue, Willy and their families and friends step off the drawing board and into a series of sparkling adventures. The letters we receive from both adults and children alike bear witness to the way in which they have come alive in people's minds and how the right combination of story and pictures can spark the imagination.

Harvey, Rue and Willy have seen us through good and bad times, have taken us across the world and have introduced us to some wonderful people in all walks of life. We are now working on a new series of *Foxwood* picture books, inspired by the countryside and wildlife around our home in Oxfordshire as well as by the adventures of our three children William, Charles and Henry.

Here are four favourite *Foxwood* titles in one beautiful Treasury. We hope you will get as much enjoyment out of reading this book as we have had putting it together.

BRIAN PATERSON

FOXWOOD TALES

THE FOXWOOD TREASURE

Harvey, Rue and Willy search for a secret recipe...

THE FOXWOOD TREASURE

The thick red jam bubbling in the old black pot had made the kitchen very hot and steamy.

Mrs Hedgehog turned to her son, Willy, who was sitting at the kitchen table staring at nothing in particular.

"What's the matter with you?" she asked irritably.

"I'm bored," he said, "there's never anything to do here."

"Never anything to do!" she said indignantly. "I've got a million and one things to do, so you can help me out."

Willy groaned. "That's not what I meant," he said.

Mrs Hedgehog took no notice. "You can take this basket of fruit and pickles and go and visit Grandpa," she went on. "That will keep you out of mischief and out of my way. Mind how you go and give him my love."

Off Willy trotted with the basket. He hadn't gone far when he met Harvey Mouse and Rue Rabbit.

"I've got to take these things to Grandpa's," he told them, "so I can't play."

"We've got nothing to do," said Rue. "Can we come with you?"

"If you'll take turns to carry the basket," answered Willy. "It's heavy and I need a rest."

They found Grandpa busy painting his old bicycle.

"Mum's sent over some pickles, Grandpa," shouted Willy.

"Oh, just the job, young Willy," replied Grandpa. Harvey and Rue were looking at the bicycle.

"Can we help you paint?" asked Harvey.

"No thanks," said Grandpa, "I've just finished it. I'm going to the meeting at Mrs Mole's house now. Would you like to come along?"

A meeting didn't sound very interesting but as there was nothing else to do they decided to go with him.

A big crowd had squeezed into Mrs Mole's front room for the meeting.

"What's it about, Grandpa?" whispered Willy.

"We need a village hall," he answered, "but funds are low so we want everyone to think of ways of raising money."

"Silence please," shouted Mr Gruffey, the badger, banging a wooden mallet on Mrs Mole's best polished table.

"Oh dear," she murmured, "the sooner we get a village hall the better."

The meeting went on a long time and Harvey, Rue and Willy were wishing they hadn't come by the time it had ended. But they did like the idea of raising money and afterwards Willy asked his grandfather what they could do to help.

"Why don't we go along to the library," said Grandpa thoughtfully, "and find out how the famous animals of Foxwood made money in the past. There are a couple of old books I would like you to read. They might give you some ideas."

"Old books," said Willy in disgust. "You can't raise money by reading old books. We want to *do* something!"

Grandpa didn't seem to hear Willy's grumble, he just gave him the names of two books and told him to ask Mrs Squirrel for them. Then he went off to arrange the next meeting with Mr Badger and Mrs Mole while the three friends settled themselves in a quiet corner of the library.

After a while Mrs Squirrel appeared with two large books, which she placed on the table in front of them. Rue took one and opened it.

"What have you got?" asked Willy, peering over Rue's shoulder.

"History," said Rue. "It's all about the famous animals who used to live in the village, Captain Weasel, Lord and Lady Moleworthy – they were very rich and lived in a mansion called Foxwood Park. Oh, here's a bit about Squire Fox…"

"I know all about him," interrupted Willy. "Grandpa told me. That's his statue in the village square."

"Everyone knows that, cleverclogs," said Rue. "What else do you know?"

"That's it really," said Willy, feeling rather squashed. He wished he'd listened more carefully when Grandpa was telling him about Foxwood in the old days.

"It says here," read Rue, "that he was a jolly chap and everyone liked him. He owned a magnificent den hidden somewhere near Foxwood and he used to invite his friends there for an evening's merry making, but he would always meet them at the edge of the wood and blindfold them before leading them to his den."

"Why, didn't he trust them?" interrupted Harvey.

"It doesn't say," went on Rue, "but apparently one dreadful night he was followed home by a gang of thieves. There was a terrific fight and he was robbed of almost everything.

He left his ruined den and built an inn called The Old Fox where he served a special lemonade made from his own secret recipe. When he died the inn was shut up and the recipe has never been found."

"That's right," interrupted Willy. "Grandpa told me where the inn was."

"If he hid the secret recipe in the inn and if we could find it, we could make a fortune," said Harvey.

"Your grandpa was right," said Rue, "the old books have given us an idea."

"Let's start looking first thing tomorrow morning," said Willy.

The next morning they met at Squire Fox's statue and headed into the woods. After searching for nearly an hour they found an overgrown path and followed it, pushing through brambles, grasses and bracken till suddenly they found themselves standing in front of a crumbling old house with an inn sign swinging crookedly from a pole above the door.

"This is it," shouted Rue, "we've found it. Give the door a good push."

They did and slowly it creaked open.

Dust and cobwebs covered everything inside and at the far end of the room stood a bar. Willy ran behind it and pulled a pump handle.

"What'll it be, gentlemen?" he asked.

"Two glasses of lemonade special, please," replied Harvey.

"That'll be 25p," said Willy, pretending to ring up the till.

"I'll be Squire Fox," said Rue. "Would you gentlemen like rooms for the night? You would? Then come this way and mind your heads."

He led the way to the stairs, followed by Harvey. Willy stayed where he was for the stairs looked rotten and they were dark.

"I think I'll wait for you down here," he said.

As soon as the others had disappeared Willy wished he had gone with them. The bar was eerie and he jumped when a board creaked.

"Who's there?" he called.

"Only me," answered a squeaky little voice, and to Willy's surprise out popped a mouse from behind the grandfather clock in the corner.

"I'm Barty," he said cheerfully, "I live here and keep the place clean. Who are you?"

"I'm Willy and I've come to look for Squire Fox's secret recipe."

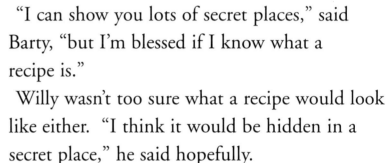

"I can show you lots of secret places," said Barty, "but I'm blessed if I know what a recipe is."

Willy wasn't too sure what a recipe would look like either. "I think it would be hidden in a secret place," he said hopefully.

"Come on, then," said Barty and joining Willy behind the bar he pulled a pump handle marked *Special.* Suddenly a tiny door opened in the biggest barrel.

"Squeeze in," said Barty, "it's quite safe." Willy stepped inside and the door slammed shut behind them.

Harvey and Rue were nosing about upstairs when they heard a door slam.

"I think we'd better see if Willy's all right," said Harvey. They ran down the stairs.

"Willy," called Rue, as they reached the bar.

No reply.

"Come on, we've got something to show you," he coaxed, thinking Willy was probably hiding for a joke.

Still no reply.

"Where on earth can he have got to?" asked Harvey. "We've only been gone a few minutes."

"I bet he's gone home," said Rue, "that door banging probably frightened him."

"If he has, he can stay there tomorrow," said Harvey crossly. "Anyway it's late so we'd better go. We'll speak to Willy in the morning."

The next morning Harvey and Rue knocked loudly on Mrs Hedgehog's door.

"Where's Willy?" Rue asked her. "We've got a bone to pick with him."

"Not here you haven't," replied Willy's mother, "because he didn't come home last night. He told me he would stay with his grandfather and that's where you'll find him now."

Rue and Harvey were becoming more and more cross with Willy for wasting so much time and when they reached Grandpa's cottage they knocked even louder on the door.

"Go away," groaned Grandpa, "it's too early to wake people."

"Tell Willy we want him," said Harvey, "then we'll go away."

"I can't do that," said Grandpa firmly, "because he's not here." And he slammed the door.

"Not here and not at home," said Harvey in dismay. "Then… Oh…no. The Old Inn. He must still be there. Quick!"

They ran all the way back to the inn and searched it from top to bottom. There was no sign of Willy. "If he doesn't show up soon," said Harvey as they walked back to the village, "we'll have to tell his mother."

There was a bench at the foot of Squire Fox's statue and Harvey and Rue sat down on it, too tired and worried to talk about what to do next. Suddenly the statue spoke.

"Is anyone there?" it asked. Harvey and Rue leapt up, terrified. Strange scratching noises came from inside the statue.

"It's haunted," cried Harvey.

"No it's not," said the statue, "it's me. I can't get out."

"That's Willy's voice," shouted Rue happily, "he's in the statue."

Then, to their amazement, they heard another voice. "There's a door here," it said. "If we push can you pull?"

Harvey and Rue prodded frantically around the base of the statue. Suddenly Rue felt a movement. "Got it," he called. "Push as hard as you can."

A stone panel opened an inch. Harvey grabbed the edge, Rue grabbed Harvey and together they tugged.

The stone flew open and Willy tumbled out onto the ground followed by Barty.

"Where on earth have you been?" asked Harvey. "We were just going to organise a search party, and who's that...?"

"It's Barty," answered Willy, "and we've found Squire Fox's den. Come on, we'll show you."

As Harvey and Rue crawled along the narrow passage they thought Willy must be braver than he seemed, for it was cold and damp and very dark. Suddenly, however, the passage opened out into a beautiful high-ceilinged hall. They stared in wonder. At last Rue spoke.

"To think it's been here in the village all this time," he said, "and no one knew. Cunning old Fox. Fox Hall!"

"Fox Hall!" echoed Harvey. "The Hall! That's it. The Village Hall. Willy, you and Barty have found the new village hall!"

"That's not all we've found," said Willy. "Look at this, it's the secret lemonade recipe. Barty lined a secret drawer in this old chest with it; he didn't know it was valuable."

"Hooray!" said Harvey. "Now you've found the recipe we can make the lemonade again. We'll make it famous and we'll be famous too."

"Not just us," said Willy thoughtfully, "it was Grandpa who gave us the book about Squire Fox."

The whole village celebrated the news that Willy and his new friend, Barty, had found Fox Hall, and at the last meeting at Mrs Mole's house they decided to re-open the Old Fox Inn with a grand party.

Grandpa made a barrel of special lemonade and animals came from far
and wide just to taste the delicious brew. The party was a huge success
and raised more than enough money to build a new entrance to Fox Hall.

Grandpa enjoyed the gala opening of the Old Fox Inn so much that he stayed on and became the best landlord the village had had since Squire Fox himself.

Willy and Barty were given the honour of cutting the ribbon at the opening of the new village hall and Barty stayed on as caretaker. Harvey and Rue weren't forgotten, either, for together with Willy and Barty they got the best reward of all. As much lemonade as they could wish for. Free for ever.

FOXWOOD TALES

THE FOXWOOD REGATTA

The day of the Foxwood Regatta is drawing near...

THE FOXWOOD
REGATTA

As Willy Hedgehog rushed up the path from the river, he caught sight of his friends Harvey Mouse and Rue Rabbit.

"Wait for me," he shouted, "something awful's happened. I've just seen the rats ram the squirrels. They're in a fast new boat and they're bound to win."

The Foxwood Regatta was only two weeks away. As usual, Harvey, Rue and Willy would be in the last race, which the rats, who were good at cheating and bullying, always won. The only rule was that your boat, which could be any kind, must be home made.

"Let them win," said Rue, "I don't think I'll bother this year."

"I agree," said Willy, "I can't swim and I hate water."

"Stop talking like that," shouted Harvey. "I'm not giving in to those sneaky rats. If you can't beat 'em, join 'em, I say."

Willy looked startled. "What do you mean?" he squeaked. "Ask for a ride in their boat?"

"No, you idiot," explained Harvey, "I mean use cunning. Find out what their plan is and make sure it doesn't work."

"How do we do that?" asked Rue.

"Spying," said Harvey, "so they can't spring any surprises."

Rue's father said they could use the old barn to build their boat. It was on the
river bank and just right for launching. They set to work cleaning and tidying it,
and were ready to begin work when an argument started. What kind of boat did
they need?

"Something strong," said Harvey, "that will smash the rats' bows if they ram us.
Remember what Willy saw yesterday."

"With extra thick planks and iron bolts," added Willy.

"Yes," agreed Rue, "and flat bottomed like a punt so it won't capsize."

"We'd never get it moving," muttered Harvey, "it's no good being unsinkable if everyone's going faster."

"What about a steam boat?" said Rue suddenly. "Plenty of power in steam."

"Less effort than rowing, too," said Willy.

"We can't build anything like that," said Harvey.

They spent so much time shouting and arguing that by the end of the day they hadn't even begun their real work. When Rue's mother arrived she was greeted by three glum faces.

"What's wrong?" she asked. "Can I help?"

"No," said Rue sadly, "we've got a good idea for a boat we can't build."

"Why not ask Captain Otter?" suggested Mrs Rabbit. "You remember, he used to run the old paddle-ferry…"

"That's it. A paddleboat," interrupted Harvey. "Thanks, Mrs Rabbit. You've probably just solved our problem."

The next day they borrowed a boat and set off to find Captain Otter.
Harvey and Rue rowed, while Willy looked out for rats. Before long he spotted
three in a very ordinary-looking boat.

"They couldn't do much harm in that, Willy," said Rue, "are you sure they
were capsizing boats yesterday?"

"Yes," said Willy thoughtfully, "but they were in a different boat and there were
more of them."

"They've disappeared in the reeds over there," said Harvey. "There must be
a hidden inlet. Let's go ashore, then we can creep up and sneak a look
at what they're doing."

Peering through the undergrowth they spied the rats fitting
sharp pointed poles into brackets fastened to the sides of a boat.

"Very clever," said Harvey, "those poles could easily make a hole in a light boat, and they're carried underwater so no one sees them."

"We were right about needing thick planks, then," said Rue, "and about needing speed."

"That's where Captain Otter can help," said Harvey. "Let's go!"

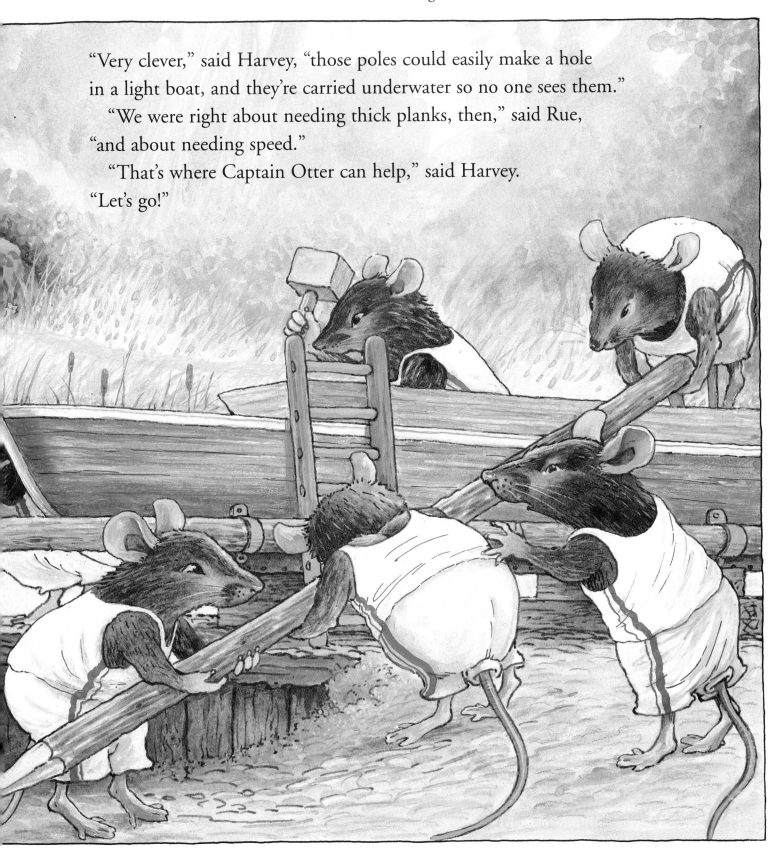

An hour later Willy, in the bows, called out, "Pull over to the bank. There's something ahead that looks like a houseboat."

It was a houseboat and, as they drew alongside, they were greeted by a cheery shout!

"It's Rue, isn't it, with some friends?" asked Captain Otter. "How's your mother, and what brings you here?"

"We need your help, sir," said Rue. "We're in for the last race in the Regatta, but we don't stand a chance if we can't outwit the rats."

"Count me in," said the Captain. "I've no time for those rascally rats, but I'm too old to take them on myself."

He invited them aboard and Rue told Captain Otter about their plan to build a paddleboat.

The Captain whistled. "It won't be easy, you know," he said.

"We'll do the work," promised Harvey, "if you'll draw the plans."

"Done," said the Captain. "Now you cut off home and I'll get to work. We'll meet again tomorrow."

As soon as Rue and his friends had gone, Captain Otter began work. It was no easy matter. Several times he had to tear up the plans and start again, but by midnight the drawings were finished, and by dawn he had built a model. After an hour or two's sleep he set out for Foxwood. Harvey, Rue and Willy couldn't wait to get started when they saw the model.

"If our boat is half as beautiful we'll be the pride of the Regatta," said Willy.

Captain Otter beamed. "We'll make the hull first," he said, "then fit the stove, the boiler and the paddles."

The three friends set to work. First they chose and shaped the planks for the hull, then Willy began nailing them together. Too eager, he hammered a nail so hard it went right through the wood, making a huge hole.

"Clumsy idiot," yelled Harvey. "If you keep bashing like that we'll end up with a sieve, not a boat."

Willy threw down the hammer in disgust. "Do it yourself, if you're so clever," he muttered, stalking off.

"You shouldn't have said that," interrupted Captain Otter. "You know how touchy Willy can be."

"Well, we can't wait all day for him to get over his sulks," sighed Rue, grabbing the hammer. "I'll finish it. He'll feel better in the morning."

Willy did feel better, and made a good job of tarring the joints. Harvey and Rue screwed down the canopy poles and Captain Otter helped them fit the rudder and build the wood store.

"Painting next," he said. "You can do that, Willy."

"Right," said Willy, beginning with a blue stripe. "Now green," he muttered, "and then red, I think."

He stepped back to admire his work and gasped! The colours had all run.

"Ah well," he said bravely as he wiped off the paint, "that's another mistake I won't make again."

Rue's father arrived with a handsome wooden figurehead and
Captain Otter fixed a shiny brass funnel. When Harvey's
mother brought a striped canopy their glorious ship was ready.

Harvey, Rue and Willy were up early next morning to help Captain Otter with the launching. Word had got about and there was quite a crowd on the bank, waiting to cheer the ship on its way.

First the Captain and Rue's father made a slipway, then everyone heaved and pushed. Slowly at first, then with a rush and a splash the paddleboat was floating proudly on the river.

Harvey, Rue and Willy climbed on board.

"Captain Otter," called Harvey, "we couldn't have built her without you. Will you name her, please?"

"That I will," answered the Captain, smiling happily. He turned to Harvey's mother.

"Have you got it?" he asked mysteriously.

"Here you are, Captain," she said, and handed him a bottle of Squire Fox's special lemonade. The Captain broke the bottle on the bows.

"I name this ship *Duchess of Foxwood*," he said, and everyone cheered. The three friends were very proud.

As Captain Otter joined Harvey, Rue and Willy for their first lesson in handling her the rats rowed slowly alongside.

"Mind you don't run out of fuel before the race," one of them jeered.

Harvey thought of their wood stacks. "No fear of that," he called, "you won't catch us running out of steam."

After supper Harvey, Rue and Willy settled on board the *Duchess* for the night. After a while Willy awoke with a start.

"Did you hear that?" he asked.

"No I didn't," said Harvey sleepily. "You must have been dreaming, Willy."

"I was dreaming about logs," Willy replied. "I do hope we have enough."

The first thing Rue heard in the morning was his mother calling them for breakfast.

Harvey peered through the porthole. "Where's Willy?" he said. "His bunk's empty."

"Probably eating breakfast," said Rue.

But he wasn't. Rue's mother said she had seen him setting off along the river bank earlier.

Just as they were starting breakfast Willy strolled in.

"Where have you been?" asked Harvey.

"Just checking the route," said Willy, holding out his plate for a large helping of Mrs Rabbit's scrambled eggs.

"We've got all day free," said Rue.

"Let's go to the fairground," suggested Harvey.

"And buy some buns," said Willy, who was always hungry.

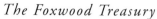

The scene was set for a wonderful day. There were flower sellers, tents, stalls, picnics and boating. Mr Mouse and Mr Rabbit tried a spot of punting, while Mr Hedgehog helped the ladies set out the picnic. Willy and Harvey enjoyed a cup of tea while keeping a close eye on Rue who was messing about on the river.

Even Mr Gruffey, the badger, was there coaching one of the crews, but,

unfortunately, his bike got a puncture.

With only a short time to go before their race, Willy sneaked off to buy more buns and by the time the Squire of Foxwood arrived at the start a large crowd had gathered.

"My stomach feels funny," said Willy.

"Too many buns," said Harvey unsympathetically.

"No," said Willy, "not buns, rats! There they are now, looking really fierce."

"Well they…" began Harvey, but he was interrupted by the Squire calling the animals to be ready for the start of the last race. Harvey, Rue and Willy hurried to untie the *Duchess* from her mooring and get her to the starting line.

"Are you ready, get set, go!" called the Squire and, with a cheer from the crowd, they were off.

The rats dug in their oars and spurted off, narrowly missing a crew of squirrels and sending their sailing dinghy so badly off course it collided with some nervous hedgehogs. A boatload of over-eager mice lost an oar but, surprisingly, the rabbits, paddling a sturdy canoe, had overtaken the rats by the time the *Duchess* had got up steam.

By the time they reached open country the boats were neck and neck. This was the rats' chance. Steering straight for the hedgehogs they upended their boat against the bank. The poor hedgehogs could only scramble ashore and watch the others go by.

"Did you see that?" shouted Willy indignantly. "Cheats!" and he hurled a sticky bun at the rat captain. Immediately a flour bomb hurtled through the air and burst on his head.

"Full steam ahead," ordered Harvey. "They're coming after us." But as he spoke the *Duchess's* engine spluttered and stopped.

"No logs left," called Rue, "the rats must…"

Crash!

"They've rammed us," said Willy, "and look, their pole's broken. Hooray!"

Rushing to the side, Harvey and Rue looked over. The rats were all shouting at once, dismayed that their secret weapon had failed.

"Head for the bank," said Willy.

"No," said Rue, "we can't give up now."

"We're not going to," said Willy, "just refuel. I stacked logs along the route this morning – just in case… I told you I heard something last night. The rats must have been emptying our store."

"Willy, you're a genius," said Harvey.

Once they had fresh logs aboard it didn't take long for the *Duchess* to catch up with the two leading boats. The rats and rabbits were level with each other with only one more bend before the finish.

"More wood," said Harvey, as Willy and Rue threw logs into the stove, "we can still do it." And the faithful *Duchess* fairly flew through the water.

Furious at having victory snatched from them by a boat they couldn't sink, the rats turned on the rabbits.

They bombarded them with flour bombs, then, when the rabbits could hardly see what they were doing, they drove their oars into the water and shot straight at their boat. There was a tremendous crash, the boat sank and the rabbits were left splashing about in the water. With a triumphant shout the rats shot ahead.

"Look!" yelled Willy. "They can't swim."

Harvey swung the *Duchess* over to the rabbits. Rue threw out ropes and they all leaned over to pull the rabbits to safety.

But it was too late to catch up. The rats would win. There would be no prize for the *Duchess* in spite of her crew's efforts.

"Poor Captain Otter," said Harvey sadly. "He did so want us to win."

"No one's cheering the rats," said Rue suddenly. "Do you think the crowd saw what happened?"

"They might have done," answered Willy. "Look, there's the finishing post, we're nearer than the rats realised."

As the rats crossed the finishing line, everyone fell silent. Then, as they grabbed the first prize, they were chased off to boos and hisses and cries of "Cheats" from the crowd.

"Well, we'll be second, anyway," said Harvey. "That's better than nothing." And, with a cheerful toot-toot, they steered the *Duchess* to the finish.

The crowd cheered as Harvey, Rue and Willy were presented with second prize and first prize for the prettiest boat on the river.

"Well done," said Captain Otter. "I saw what happened and you're the real winners, to my mind. I don't think the rats will dare to enter next year!"

"I hope they will," said Harvey, "we can beat them if you help."

"Count on me," said the Captain. "Now, let's celebrate. Sticky buns and lemonade all round."

FOXWOOD TALES

THE FOXWOOD SMUGGLERS

A day at the seaside turns into high adventure…

THE FOXWOOD SMUGGLERS

The door of Mr Gruffey's shop clanged open.

"Three glasses of special lemonade, please," shouted Willy Hedgehog, pushing past his friends, Harvey Mouse and Rue Rabbit.

"You'll be lucky," snapped Mr Gruffey.

Willy was taken aback. "What do you mean?" he asked.

Mr Gruffey leaned forward. "I mean," he said, "that there isn't any."

"But there's always special lemonade," complained Willy.

"Not today there isn't. There isn't any lemonade and there aren't any vegetables. And there aren't any because they've been stolen," said Mr Gruffey. "Grandpa Hedgehog and I have sat up for the last three nights trying to catch the thieves in the act…"

"Why haven't you, then?" interrupted Rue. He was as thirsty as Willy.

"Well, because…because it's not as easy to keep awake as we thought," answered Mr Gruffey sheepishly.

Willy's temper was on the boil. "You're supposed to give us free lemonade whenever we want it," he reminded Mr Gruffey rudely. "So what are you going to do about that?"

"Nothing," retorted Mr Gruffey. "I'm going on holiday. My caravan needs a good clean and a new coat of paint. It'll take me at least a week to get it straight and there's no point in staying here because Grandpa Hedgehog and I will never catch these ruffians on our own."

Harvey was looking thoughtful. "Mr Gruffey," he said, "if we come and work on the caravan with you, we'll get it done quicker, and then we can help you try to trap the thieves."

Mr Gruffey didn't answer. In fact he didn't seem to have heard, but just wandered round the shop picking up bits of rubbish.

"All right," he said at last. "Just this once, but don't think you can make a habit of it, and…" he glared at them…"make sure your parents know what you're up to."

"Brilliant, Harvey," laughed Willy as they left the shop. "Fancy old Gruffey agreeing to your plan."

"It won't take long to slap a dash of paint on that caravan," said Rue, "then we'll have the rest of the time to ourselves…a free holiday by the sea."

"Hang on," said Harvey, "we've still got to ask our parents."

Willy had no doubts. "My mum and dad'll let me go," he said, "they never mind what I do as long as I tell them where I am."

He waved goodbye, in a hurry to tell his parents and get his packing done.

"See you at the station," called Harvey as the other two ran off. "And don't be late."

The next morning Willy was the last to arrive, trailing what looked like all his belongings. Harvey stared at him in dismay.

"I wish your mum and dad had said no," he wailed, squeezing Willy and his packages into the carriage. "Come on."

"Come on, settle down," said Mr Gruffey. "We've got a long journey ahead of us."

He was much more cheerful away from the shop, and even helped Willy stow his luggage on the rack. The guard blew his whistle and the Foxwood train steamed slowly out of the station.

Rue borrowed Willy's telescope and pointed it out of the
window as the little train gathered speed and headed
into the country. Mr Gruffey settled down to read his
paper, and Willy climbed up to the rack, searching
through his luggage till he found a small packet of
sandwiches.

"Is there ever a time when you're not hungry?" asked
Harvey.

"I get travel sick," answered Willy, "and eating helps."

"Look," shouted Rue suddenly, pointing with the telescope at a boat sailing down
the river towards the estuary. "Rats!"

"Bet they're up to no good," said Willy, brushing away crumbs.

"Oh, I don't know," said Mr Gruffey kindly, "even the rats might just be enjoying
a sail on such a glorious day."

The journey went on and on, and
Willy began to fidget. "When do
we get there?" he asked.

"Not long now," said Mr Gruffey.
"It's the next stop. If you look out
of the window you'll catch a
glimpse of the sea."

Willy took his telescope and
spotted a lighthouse. Then, "Look
at all the water," he shouted.
"Yippee! This is going to be the
best holiday ever."

Mr Gruffey helped them down with the luggage as the train pulled into the station. "Wait till it stops," he shouted. "I don't want any accidents."

Harvey, Rue and Willy ignored him. They pushed and shoved, determined to be the first off.

Mr Gruffey sighed. "Perhaps I should have come on my own," he muttered. "I'm not used to this."

"Is it far?" asked Willy, wishing he hadn't brought quite so much luggage. "Only you see, my little legs get tired quickly."

"Shut up, Willy," said Rue. "You're always moaning, and if you're not moaning, you're eating. You're a bore!"

Willy stuck his tongue out. "Bore yourself," he said.

"That's enough," said Mr Gruffey briskly. "Come along. It's this way." He pointed to a cliff path winding down to the beach.

"What a view," Harvey called out. "I've never seen anything like it."

"There's that lighthouse again," said Willy. "Can we go and explore it?"

"After we've been to the caravan," said Mr Gruffey firmly. "There it is."

"What *that*?" gasped Rue.

"He did say it needed knocking into shape," said Harvey.

"Knocking down, you mean," whispered Willy.

They spent the afternoon cleaning, polishing and dusting till their arms were almost dropping off.

"That's more like it," said Mr Gruffey at last, pleased with their hard work. "Now we can unpack, make the beds up, and have supper. Tomorrow we'll start on the outside."

They discussed the work that had to be done the next day as they tucked into one of Mr Gruffey's succulent pies. Willy managed several helpings. "I think I've eaten too much," he said, hoping to get out of the washing up.

Mr Gruffey smiled. He was getting to know Willy. "You can dry up," he said, "that's easier."

"Will you tell us a story in bed?" asked Harvey, as they put on their pyjamas.

"Well now, let's think," said the old badger. "Did I ever tell you about the ghost of Lighthouse Rock? It's a true story and, as I remember it, it goes like this..."
It was a good story and they wanted to hear it all, but by the time Mr Gruffey had got to the end, Harvey, Rue and Willy, tired out with hard work and sea air, were fast asleep.

When the three friends woke the next morning the sun was shining and bacon was sizzling in the pan.

"I'm starving," said Willy, jumping out of bed and washing and dressing as quickly as possible.

"Ready for work?" asked Mr Gruffey.

"Can't wait!" said Willy.

"Good," said Mr Gruffey. "The sooner we start the sooner we finish and you can go off by yourselves."

Mr Gruffey put on his old beach hat and jacket. He opened the paint pots and gave them each a brush. They worked so well that by mid-day the job was finished.

Mr Gruffey could hardly believe it. "Well done!" he exclaimed. "I never thought you'd stick it, but I was wrong. I think we've earned some lunch, don't you?"

"It's good to relax when you've finished a job," said Mr Gruffey, happily. "Now, what have you three got planned for the rest of the day?"

"Not quite sure yet," said Harvey. "But wherever we go we'll be back in time for supper."

"You bet," said Willy.

There was so much to do on the beach they forgot all about the time.

"This is the life," said Rue, digging his toes into the soft sand.

"Anyone for a swim?" asked Willy, who had got as far as paddling.

"I'd rather explore the rock pools," said Harvey.

"Me too," said Rue, and they ran off.

"Wait for me," shouted Willy. "I might drown."

Fresh
Cockles·Mussels

After the rock pools they built a huge sandcastle.

"Now what?" said Harvey. It was still quite light.

Willy looked across at the lighthouse. "That!" he said. "Let's explore that."

"It's haunted," Rue reminded them. "Remember Mr Gruffey's story?"

"I don't believe it," said Willy. "He was just trying to frighten us.

How do we get across, though?"

At that moment a small rabbit came up to Rue. "Excuse me," she said, "but I couldn't help overhearing. My uncle keeps his boats over there. I'm sure it would be all right to borrow one if you leave him a note."

Rue thanked her and they clambered aboard.

"This is fun," giggled Willy. "Come on, you two, row."

"Don't boss," said Rue. "You ought to take a turn."

"Can't," said Willy. "I'm looking out for pirates," and he scanned the horizon with his telescope.

Just as they reached the deep channel between the shore and the lighthouse, Harvey yelled, "Water's coming in."

"A leak," groaned Rue. "Can we make the island?"

"No," said Harvey. "It's coming in fast."

"We'll have to swim for it," said Rue. "Jump, Willy!"

Once in the water, Rue grabbed an oar and held on to it, while Harvey grabbed Willy and the other oar.

"Are there sharks in these waters?" Willy asked miserably.

"Never mind about sharks," said Harvey, "just make for the island."

It seemed ages before they got there, but at last they clambered out onto the rocks. Shaking, and soaking wet, they sat down to recover their breath.

"Sorry," sobbed Willy, "we should never have come."

"My fault," said Rue. "I chose the boat."

"Never mind whose fault it is," said Harvey. "We're safe. That's all that matters."

Willy stared at the towering, crumbling lighthouse.

"It does look haunted," he said. "I don't think I want to explore it after all."

"We've got to go to the top," said Rue. "It's our only hope of spotting a rescue ship."

"No one's going to rescue us, because no one knows we're here," said Willy, really frightened now.

"You never know," said Rue. "Come on, I'll lead the way. The handrail's loose, so be careful."

"If I'd known it was so high I'd have stayed at home," panted Willy, as they neared the top. "We must have climbed hundreds of steps."

"Ssh! Quiet! I can hear something," said Rue suddenly.

"The ghost..." whispered Willy.

"There it is again," said Rue. He could hear voices now and they were getting closer.

"That's no ghost, it's the rats," cried Willy. "I'd know them anywhere. I knew someone would rescue us."

"Quiet a minute, Willy," said Harvey. "I don't trust them. Let's see if we can hear what they're up to."

The leader of the rats was talking. "A very nice little haul," he said. "A dozen crates of lemonade and several boxes of mixed veg. Let's get going. We'll collect them for market first thing in the morning."

Harvey, Rue and Willy could hardly believe their ears. As soon as the coast was clear they hurried down to check the rats' cargo.

"Look," said Willy, "Grandpa Hedgehog's special lemonade and…these must be Mr Gruffey's vegetables. We've caught the robbers red-handed."

"A fat lot of good that will do us," said Rue. "Stuck here."

"At least we won't starve," said Willy.

"Very funny," said Rue, "but we've *got* to find a way off."

Meanwhile, at the caravan, it was well past supper time and Mr Gruffey was getting worried. "They should have been back ages ago," he muttered.

There was a knock at the door. Mr Gruffey gave a sigh of relief. "That must be them now."

But it wasn't. "Anyone there?" called a familiar voice.

"Captain Otter!" said Mr Gruffey. "Come in, my friend. What brings you here?"

"Fine weather and a southerly breeze. It's been a splendid day for sailing and I'm moored in the bay. Just thought I'd drop in."

"Well, I'm glad you're here," said Mr Gruffey, and he went on to tell him how worried he was.

"We'll search down the coast at once," said Captain Otter. "They can't have gone far, but we'd best get a move on before the light goes."

On the island, the three friends were still wondering how to escape.

"I've got an idea," said Willy. "I read in a book that someone who was stuck on an island burned a fire, night and day, to attract passing ships."

"Did it work?" asked Harvey eagerly.

"I don't know," said Willy. "I didn't finish it."

"Idiot," said Rue.

"It's a good idea, whether he finished the book or not," said Harvey. "Let's get a fire going now. If this place is really haunted we don't want to spend the night here."

Willy was nearly crying. "I hope Mr Gruffey will come," he said. Then he brightened. "We could look for firewood while we wait."

They did their best but had only a small pile when Willy suddenly pointed to the shore. "Look," he screamed, "a boat," and gave a little dance of joy, until a thought struck him and he stopped, frozen to the spot. "What if it's the rats," he said in a small voice. "We'd come off worse in a fight." He handed the telescope to Rue. "You look," he begged. "I'm too scared."

"I've seen that boat before," said Rue. "Yes, it's the *Seamaid*."

They scrambled down the rocks, waving and shouting.

"Catch," called Captain Otter, throwing a rope. "Glad to see you."

"Same here," said Willy. "And we've got something to show you."

As soon as Captain Otter and Mr Gruffey were ashore they all went back to the lighthouse.

"No doubt about whose lemonade and vegetables they are," declared Mr Gruffey. "We'd better get them aboard quickly. Those rats are cunning. They may easily have a lookout posted on the mainland who will have already spotted us."

Mr Gruffey was right. As Willy turned his telescope to the shore he saw the rats' sailing barge approaching.

"Quick!" shouted Mr Gruffey. "If we hurry we can still load up and get off in time."

"We'll never make it," said Willy. "They're coming fast."

They heaved, pushed and pulled until they were exhausted, then, "Ready or not, I'm casting off," called Captain Otter. "The rats are almost on us."

Mr Gruffey climbed aboard. Harvey and Rue jumped. "Come on, Willy, lad, jump," encouraged Mr Gruffey. Willy did, but missed his footing, and fell into the sea.

"Go on without me," he spluttered. "I'm done for."

"No, you're not," shouted the Captain, throwing him a rope.

There was a sudden thump and everyone fell forward. The rats' barge rammed *Seamaid*.

"She's strong, don't worry," said Captain Otter, as the others hauled in a rather soggy Willy. Then he hurled *Seamaid's* anchor at the rats' ship. Crash! A large hole appeared in her side, water poured in and she sank.

"Leave them," said Mr Gruffey, as the rats bobbed to the surface. "They're good swimmers."

The wind caught *Seamaid*'s sails and she was off.

"It's their turn to be marooned," said Harvey with satisfaction. "They won't trouble us for a while."

Willy turned to his friends with tears in his eyes. "Thanks for saving my life," he mumbled.

"We couldn't leave you to the sharks," said Harvey, and everyone laughed.

They dried off by the ship's stove, laughing and joking as they sailed peacefully back to the harbour.

"I won't ever forget this day," said Willy quietly, "and I'm glad it's ended so happily."

By the time they got back to the caravan, the supper was rather burnt, but it didn't stop them enjoying every mouthful.

"Grandpa Hedgehog will be glad of our news," said Rue.

"So was I," said Mr Gruffey. "This has been a very special holiday. My caravan is newly painted, and I've got fresh vegetables to sell. Yes, it's turned out very well. Everyone is safe and we're free of the Foxwood Smugglers." He raised his glass, and they all joined in a toast. "To Foxwood."

FOXWOOD TALES

THE FOXWOOD SURPRISE

It's Christmas time at Foxwood...

THE FOXWOOD SURPRISE

"**I**s Harvey at home?" asked Willy Hedgehog, kicking snow from his wellingtons.

"He's upstairs with Rue," said Mrs Mouse. "Go and see what they're up to, Willy. They're making an awful noise."

"There you are, Willy," said Rue as Willy opened the door. "And about time. We've finished our toboggans and nearly done yours."

"Thanks," said Willy. "But I haven't been wasting my time. I've done our Christmas present list."

"Don't talk about Christmas presents," groaned Harvey. "We've no money left. You know how much the stuff for the toboggans cost."

"Let's earn some, then," said Willy.

"How?" asked Harvey and Rue together.

"Carol singing?" suggested Willy. "It's Christmas, isn't it?"

"I can't sing for toffee," muttered Rue.

"Not toffee, money." Willy could never resist a joke.

"Oh, shut up, Willy," snapped Rue. "This is no time for feeble jokes."

Willy was just about to answer when Harvey stopped him. "Carol singing's not a bad idea, Willy," he said. "Let's start tonight."

That evening, well wrapped up and carrying lanterns and sheets of music, the three friends met outside Mr Gruffey's shop. It was shut.

"He's locked up early because of the snow," said Rue, reading a note pinned to the door.

"There's plenty more places," said Willy cheerfully. "Let's try Mrs Mole next."

But Mrs Mole's house was in darkness, and so were the next three houses they tried. By the time they got to Mrs Squirrel's they were almost ready to give up.

"What shall we sing first?" said Willy, shuffling the sheets in his hand.

"That's just it," said Harvey. "We're not organised. We don't know what to sing and we don't know who's at home. You shouldn't have been in such a hurry, Willy."

"I wasn't," shouted Willy. "You were the one who wanted to start tonight."

The window above them flew open. "Stop that noise," called Mrs Squirrel.
"You'll wake my babies."

"That settles it," said Harvey. "The first house with someone at home
and she tells us to shut up. I'm going home."

"Hang on," said Willy. "Don't go yet. I've got a brilliant idea."

"Not another one," said Rue. He shrugged. "Well, let's hear it."

"It's the new squire at the Old Manor House," said Willy. "Squire Fox. Everyone says he's very rich."

"That's right," said Harvey, seeing Willy's idea. "Dad says he's rolling in it."

"Rolling in what?" asked Rue. He had no idea what Harvey and Willy were talking about.

"Money, you fool," said Willy. "If we play our cards right we might get all we need from him."

"Unless he's out…" muttered Rue.

"It's worth a try," insisted Willy.

Half an hour later they reached the Manor House.

"I hope you're right, Willy," said Harvey doubtfully, untying the rusty chain round the gates. "It looks deserted to me."

Willy wasn't listening. "Some place," he muttered, holding the lantern high. "You'd have to be rich to live in a house like this."

"It gives me the creeps," said Rue.

They climbed the steps to the front door and Rue banged the knocker loudly.

"Let's get started," said Willy. "And sing up, so they can hear us."

They were heard all right. Before they had finished the first verse the door creaked open and a stout badger in a smart uniform glared out at them.

"Go away," he snarled. "You've no business to come snooping round other people's houses. Don't let me catch you here again until..." He stopped suddenly and slammed the door.

The three friends were speechless. "He didn't give us a chance!" said Willy at last. "Our singing wasn't that bad."

"It wasn't the singing," said Harvey thoughtfully. "They just don't want visitors. Did you notice all the windows were shuttered?"

"I told you the place gives me the creeps," said Rue.

"I bet Squire Fox told him to get rid of us," panted Willy as they ran down the path.

All the way home Willy kept on and on about the squire's meanness. "He won't go without at Christmas," he grumbled. "As long as he's got enough for himself, he'll never think about Foxwood."

"You're jealous," said Rue.

"I'm not," said Willy, "I just wish my plan had worked, that's all."

Harvey yawned. "I don't want anything at the moment," he said, "except my bed and no more carol singing."

"What about taking the toboggans to the woods tomorrow and collecting bundles of firewood to sell?" said Rue.

"Good idea," said Harvey.

"Don't forget to bring string," called Willy, as each trudged off wearily to his own home.

The next morning, after a good hot breakfast, the three friends set off for the woods, each pulling his toboggan. Willy's mum had given him a loaf of bread and a flask of soup.

"That will keep you all going," she said, as she waved him off.

Willy's legs were so short and the snow was so deep that he soon felt tired. Harvey and Rue kindly took it in turns to pull his toboggan and give him a ride on one of theirs. When they reached the wood Rue was all for getting to work at once.

"Shall we eat first?" suggested Willy hopefully. "Mum has put soup and a fresh loaf in the hamper."

Harvey and Rue were easily persuaded, so they found a sheltered spot and shared out the picnic.

"I could work all night now," said Rue happily, when the last crumb had gone.

Harvey, Rue and Willy soon had their toboggans piled high with neatly tied bundles.

"That's the last of the string," said Rue. "We'd better be getting home."

"It should fetch a fair price," said Willy, already thinking about what he could buy with his share.

The laden toboggans were heavy to pull. By the time they reached the edge of the wood Willy's legs were aching. He was thinking longingly of his earlier rides, when, suddenly, he heard a loud cry.

The cry echoed again through the tall, bare trees.

"Listen," said Willy. "I thought I heard someone call 'Help'."
At that moment they saw a small badger running towards them.
"There's been an accident," he called breathlessly. "Please come."

Harvey, Rue and Willy followed the little badger out of the wood.
Suddenly Willy stumbled on a snow-covered log and landed in front of
a carriage that had skidded off the road, and was hanging over the
edge, above a sheer drop to the icy river below. Two horses
stood shivering in the shafts.

"Is anyone hurt?" gasped Willy, as the others came hurrying up.

A tall fox appeared from behind the carriage, dusting the snow from an expensive-looking coat. "We're unharmed but a little shaken," he said calmly.

Rue freed the horses, while Harvey comforted the coachman. Willy wanted to know what had happened.

"Icy roads," said the fox. "The horses slipped on a bad patch and before we knew what was happening the coach was half over."

The coachman scratched his head. "The problem is," he asked, "how do we get it back?"

"I think I know," said Willy. He beckoned to the little badger. "Come
with me. I'll need help."

"What's he up to now?" asked Rue.

"I've a horrible feeling I know," said Harvey a few minutes later, as Willy and
his new friend appeared, pulling the three toboggans.

"What are you going to do, Willy?" asked Rue anxiously.

"Use the wood from the toboggans to make planks for the carriage wheels
to grip on."

"But we spent hours making them," protested Rue, "and the wood took
all our money."

"I know, but it's the only way," said Willy firmly.

They set to work, pulling strips of wood from the toboggans and forcing them
under the wheels.

"This had better work," Harvey told Willy, "or you're for it."

Everyone worked hard. First they scraped the snow from under the carriage, then Willy laid a line of toboggan planks under the wheels. The fox and the coachman brought some strong branches from the wood to use as levers.

When all was ready everyone pushed and heaved till, with one final effort, the carriage stood upright, its wheels resting on the planks. The footman roped the horses to the back, and with much coaxing persuaded them to pull the old coach slowly back on to the road.

"Brilliant, Willy," said the fox. "We'd have been stuck without your help." Then his eye caught the splintered wood lying in the snow. "Sorry about your toboggans."

"They were new," Willy said. "I don't think Harvey and Rue are very pleased with me."

"I was on my way to shop in town," went on the fox briskly. "Hop aboard, everybody, and we'll mix business with pleasure. It seems I've one or two things to add to my shopping list."

"There's no point in our coming," said Harvey. "We've no money. That's why we were collecting wood to sell."

"We wouldn't mind the ride, though," said Willy quickly.

When everybody had settled down, the fox said suddenly, "Your little friend's going off."

"We don't know him," said Rue. "We thought he was with you. He raised the alarm, so he's the one you really ought to thank."

The fox jumped down, ran after the little badger and, after a few minutes' talk, they came back together.

As they drove into town they
discovered their new friend's name
was Jeremy, that his parents were dead,
and that he lived on his own in the wood.

"You must be very lonely," said Willy.
"Why don't you come and live with us? My mum
won't mind, and anyway you're too small to eat much."

Jeremy smiled. "Thanks," he said.

"This is great," said Harvey happily, as the carriage bowled
along. "Now I know what it feels like to be a prince."

The fox was enjoying himself too. "How about singing some carols?" he suggested. "After all, it is Christmas."

"Don't talk about carols," muttered Willy. "We went to sing carols to the squire at the Manor House yesterday. He's horribly mean, not a bit like you. His butler slammed the door in our faces."

The fox smiled. "Not all foxes are mean, you know."

"Oh, I didn't mean that," said Willy blushing, "but..."

"Just keep quiet, Willy," said Rue, "you've said enough."

When they reached the town, the fox gave them some money for Christmas shopping. "I've got some business to do," he said. "We'll meet at the old tea rooms at 5 o'clock."

The four friends looked at the money in their hands and
then at each other.

"We'll be able to buy an awful lot with this," said Rue, breaking the silence.

"Let's split up," said Harvey. "Some of my presents are secret."

"O.K.," said Willy, guessing one of them might be for him. "But I'll keep Jeremy
with me in case he gets lost."

The fox was the first to arrive at the old tea rooms, and he had already ordered by the time Willy arrived, followed by Rue and Harvey.

"Where's Jeremy?" asked Rue as they sat down.

"We got separated in one of the shops," said Willy, looking rather sheepish. "I didn't look for him because I thought he would come straight here."

"It's getting dark," said the fox, "so I'd better go and find him. You three stay here, eat your tea, and don't wander off."

"That fox bothers me," said Harvey, as they ate their scones. "Why haven't we seen him before?"

"He's rich and he's generous," said Willy.

"But where does he live?" asked Harvey.

"Well, rich people live in large houses," said Rue.

"Precisely," said Harvey. "Manor houses!"

Willy choked on his teacake. "You mean he's Squire Fox," he gasped. "And I went on about the Squire being miserable and mean. I never thought… What am I going to do?"

At that moment the fox returned, carrying a very tired Jeremy. "I found him fast asleep under the Christmas tree in the square," he said.

"Eat up now, it's getting late and I want to get you all safely home."

Willy stood up and faced the fox. "Sir," he said bravely, "or rather, Squire. I have some apologising to do. I didn't mean to call you names, and I had no idea you were the new Squire. You are, aren't you?" he added hastily.

"You're forgiven, Willy," smiled the Squire. "And I've got some explaining of my own to do. I'll tell you all about it on the way home."

On the way back to Foxwood, Squire Fox stopped the carriage and everyone picked holly and mistletoe for the Manor House.

"What a splendid squire he is," said Willy as he and Jeremy walked home.

"One of the best," agreed Jeremy.

"And what a surprise his news will be to the village," said Willy. "I don't know how we'll keep the secret till tomorrow. Come on, Jeremy," he finished. "Let's introduce you to my mum."

Willy's mother watched them from the kitchen window, struggling up the path with armfuls of parcels and wondered where they had come from.

"Hi, Mum," said Willy as she opened the door. "This is Jeremy."

"My goodness, what a surprise," said Mrs Hedgehog. "Come in, Jeremy, and welcome. Why don't you sit yourselves by the fire while I get the supper, then you can tell me what you've been up to all day."

They both sat in the most comfortable chair they could find and warmed themselves whilst they waited for Willy's mum to return from the kitchen.

But supper came too late. Willy and Jeremy fell asleep by the warm fire and Mr Hedgehog carried them up to bed.

Next morning, Willy shook Jeremy awake. "Christmas Eve," he said. "The day we wrap up all our presents and put them under the tree."

"Great," said Jeremy. "A real family Christmas."

Mrs Hedgehog heard this remark. "I hope you'll enjoy being with us, Jeremy," she said. "And stay as long as you want."

While they were eating breakfast the town crier came by. "Oh yez! Oh yez!" he called. "The new squire invites everyone to a Christmas Eve Fancy Dress Party at the Manor House. 5.30 sharp!"

"Hurray," shouted Willy. "The secret's out."

"You mean you know about this, Willy," gasped his mother. "And you managed to keep the secret."

"It's a long story," said Willy, "and there's no time to tell you now because we've got to get our costumes ready."

The whole evening was a huge success. There were party games,
prizes and sleigh rides round the grounds.

The food and drink were so good that Willy soon
had to admit that he couldn't eat any more.

At the end of the evening the Squire had two surprises left. He called Harvey, Rue, Willy and Jeremy outside. There in the snow stood a wonderful toboggan big enough for four.

"It's yours," he said, "you've earned it."

He turned to Jeremy. "It's no good having a share in the toboggan if you're not here. So what do you say to coming to live with us at the Manor House?"

"Agreed," shouted Harvey, Rue and Willy together.

Jeremy smiled, and nodded happily.